BARGAIN PRINCESS

BARGAIN PRINCESS

A Space Operetta

by Peyton Reese

Editorial review by Annette Saarinen

/ / /

What's a Space Operetta?

Wikipedia defines a space opera as "a subgenre of science fiction that often emphasizes romantic, often melodramatic adventure, set mainly or entirely in outer space, usually involving conflict between opponents possessing advanced abilities, (sci-fi) weapons, and other (sci-fi) technology."

Wikipedia defines an operetta as "a genre of light opera, light in terms both of music and subject matter."

No, there's no singing in this space operetta.

/ / /

Special thanks ...

To all of the Roses, for your encouragement and support.

DAY 1 - LANDFALL

They warned us our landing on Tashara would be rough, and they were right. The planet's electromagnetic rocks and blowing sand played havoc with our instruments, sending our landing craft pitching and yawing so bad I thought I was going to lose my breakfast. Evans finally shut off the autolander, thank God, and took us in on visual-only. He skimmed a sea of boulders, found a clear patch of gravel, and set the craft down nice and sweet.

The planet's weird electromagnetics are why our ship's sensors couldn't track, and then couldn't find, Kozlowski. We'd sent Koz and Bahktovar and six others to different corners of the planet to find friendly—or at least not too *un*friendly—tribes with whom the Federation could establish relations. It was a daunting task, considering there are over two hundred identified tribes on three major landmasses on a planet nearly as large as Earth. Our job, or should I say Commander Phillips' job, was to keep track of them, guide them, and keep them out of danger as best we could from an altitude of 30,000 kilometers. Piece of cake, right? Well, it would be, except for that shifting electromagnetic noise from the planet's surface.

The optimists in Phillips' team hoped that we'd simply lost contact with Kozlowski, that he was still alive and researching down there. The pessimists were, thankfully, quiet about what the other alternative was. Me, I was hoping he was still alive and we could find him, because he owed me fifty bucks.

Commander Phillips pulled Bahktovar out of the foothills on another corner of Tashara to guide our landing party—Evers, Chi, Bahktovar and me—to search for Kozlowski. Koz and Bahkti and the six others are like chameleons—drop them next to some civilization, and with just a week or two of observation, they can blend in to the local population like they're natives. That's a pretty useful skill when you've got that many tribes, most of which are at war with each other.

Oh, me? I'm Lieutenant Commander Baker of the Federation Star Service. I've been running security for missions like this for longer than I care to admit.

Anyway, back to the story.

We unloaded our gear from the landing craft, sent it back up to the ship (can't leave advanced technology just lying around, can we?) and started our search. We got lucky and found the tear-off lid of an MRE after just an hour of spiral searching. This, plus the partial tracking data we had on Koz from before he went missing, plus a survey of the nearby terrain, gave us a general idea of where he might have been headed, so that's the direction we headed, too.

Evers and Chi worked their tracking equipment, Bahkti watched the trail, and I watched the surrounding terrain. Sure, it was like looking for a needle in a 100-kilometer haystack, but our team was good, despite the bad electromagnetics. And by good, I mean when the sand stopped blowing for a minute, we found a piece of foil half the size of a fingertip at a distance of fifty meters. It was just a bit of a wrapper off of a wintergreen mint, Kozlowski's favorite. And it wasn't the only one—we found another one just like it about a kilometer farther down the trail, and another one a kilometer after that.

Thanks, Koz, I said to no one. Carrying foil-wrapped mints on a primitive planet like this was no way to blend in, but if it meant we could find him and pull him to safety, that was just fine with me.

We kept following the foil until the sun touched the western horizon. Our mission briefing warned us that temperatures would fall to near freezing, and Bahkti confirmed this. We could have kept going in the dark, what with our sensors and night vision, but our suits need sunlight to maintain their charge, and I didn't want us getting into some situation without fully powered armor.

/ / /

DAY 2 - ENCOUNTER

I woke the next morning to find Chi and Bahkti already scanning the horizon in the faint light of dawn. They turned to me, and Chi said, "We don't like it. We think we're not alone."

If Chi says she doesn't like something, that's good enough for me. Her intuition has saved my bacon more times than I care to admit.

I asked, "What do the scanners show?"

"Nothing. Too much background noise."

"Your recommendation?"

"Keep going, and hope the scanners pick up whatever it is before it's too late."

"Sounds like a plan." I turned to Evers, still sleeping like a baby, and kicked his boot.

We followed the trail along a dry creekbed for most of the morning, then Chi stopped. I strained to see anything in the rocks ahead, but couldn't. Evers and I joined her to see what her sensors had picked up.

"Life forms in the rocks ahead. Could be three, could be more, hiding."

"Ditto," confirmed Evers. "Metal, too. Could be swords, guns, something like that."

Bahkti said, "The tribes have single-shot percussion weapons. Some may be rifles."

"Okay," I said. "A-line. Bahkti, you stay behind us. If we go to tri, make sure you're in the middle."

"Got it."

Our armored suits are pretty strong on the front side, and cover better than Bahkti's endosuit. Our A-line formation would provide a wall of protection for him. If things got really dicey and we got surrounded, the tri-corner formation would keep our front armor on the outside, our lighter back armor inside, and Bahkti protected in the middle.

"Stun five," I ordered. "We don't know that they're dangerous, or even that they're the enemy. And hold your fire."

"Copy," said three voices simultaneously. We adjusted our blasters, lowered our visors, and started slowly forward.

Chi whispered, "Three ahead, and more in the rocks to the right."

"Copy. Hold fire."

Maniacal screams filled the air as three black-cloaked wraiths leapt from the rocks. I saw muzzle flashes and felt a bullet hit my breastplate. "Hold," I said, guessing that if Chi or Evers had been hit, they were in no worse shape than I was.

The tribals dropped their guns, drew swords, and charged us. There a chance those blades could find weak spots in our armor, so I gave the order to fire. The three tribals flew off their feet like they'd run into tree branches.

The silence felt strangely anticlimactic.

Evers said, "Six, seven, eight, hiding in the rocks."

"Ditto," confirmed Chi.

We turned our blasters toward the rocks and waited.

After a respectful silence, a hand raised from within the rocks. An open, empty hand. A slender hand. *Female,* I thought. The wrist bore a leather bracelet. The forearm was bare down to where it disappeared into a loose, dark green sleeve.

Okay, no weapon so far.

The matching left hand appeared as well, equally braceleted, and equally unarmed.

I was just thinking there should be a head in between those arms, when a hood rose just where I expected it. Then the whole ensemble slowly rose—uplifted, empty hands, long dark green cloak, slender form, unmistakably female.

Now if you're thinking that I'm holding fire because it's a female, you're right. Combat exercises have proven that over and over again—that I'm slow to fire if the target is female. It's even written up as a warning in my personnel file. That's why I picked Chi for the team—because she covers my faults. Chi will toast this native bitch if she as much as squints wrong.

"Hold," I repeated.

Chi also knows what I'm thinking, or not thinking, which is why she now reminded me, "Seven more in the rocks, boss."

"Copy."

The native paused during this time, as if to see if she would be shot. She wasn't, so she started to make her way toward us over the rocks, and when she reached the sandy ground before us, she stopped.

Still we waited, blasters leveled at her.

Ever so slowly, she brought her fingers to the side of her hood, then she peeled the hood back.

My breath caught at her beauty. And then I got ahold of myself, and I asked myself, *Now is she really that beautiful? Sure she's got perfect dark eyes, perfect cheek bones, skin the color of warm clay, full reddish-brown lips, and long, straight, black hair...*

Chi's voice interrupted my thoughts. "You're drooling, Boss."

For an instant I believed her, but then I realized she hadn't even looked at me, and couldn't see inside my visor anyway. Like I said, she just knows what I'm thinking most of the time. Bless her twitchy little trigger finger.

The native reached slowly for the clasp of her cloak. Chi said, "Could have a weapon under there."

"Not metal, not stone," came Evers' voice. He must have checked his sensors.

The cloak opened, and it slid down the native's bare arms, then dropped to the ground. No, there was no weapon in there, other than herself. No metal and no stone, that's for sure. Just a sinewy, sleek, slender form posing as if for a bathing suit competition.

I blinked a couple of times just to make sure my eyes hadn't popped out, and I closed my mouth to make sure it wasn't drooling.

She stood there, showing herself off as she eyed each of us in turn—showing herself off like one of those twentieth-century beauty contestants, except she wasn't wearing a white bathing suit, it was a dark green one. A one-piece, knit of some coarse, shiny string, with a few shiny metal rings protruding along the edges.

Chi's voice broke into my thoughts again. "You want me to zap her, boss, until your brain is working again?"

"Uh, no, hold."

Bahkti's voice broke in now. "Perhaps I should explain. In addition to showing that she is unarmed, she is demonstrating her worth. She is showing that she is worth more alive than dead."

Oh, yeah, and it's working.

During this exchange, the native had turned slowly around, to show herself from every angle. Again I couldn't help thinking, *just like a bathing suit competition.*

Now she stopped, facing me, eyeing me. Could she know what I was thinking? She'd have to be brainless not to. And she certainly had enough brains to know what she was doing and how to do it.

But now she smiled, and began to lower herself until she was kneeling, and then she leaned slowly forward with her hands behind her, until her forehead touched the sand, and then she lifted herself up enough to look into my visor again, and she said, "Ik ya panetting." And there she knelt, waiting for a response from me.

Bahkti spoke. "She says, 'I am your possession,' or 'I am your plaything.' The words are very similar."

"Well, fine," I thought, half-aloud.

I heard Bahkti say, "Keh hai."

Surprised, I half turned to him. "What did you say?"

"I said, 'yes, fine.'"

Shit! "Bahkti, don't translate everything I say!"

"Sorry, boss."

Apparently my words—or Bahkti's words—were just what this native woman wanted to hear. She rose in one smooth motion and strutted over to the three fallen native males. (Yeah, I'd forgotten about them too!) She lowered herself to one knee, picked up the nearest knife, and slit the throat of the first one. She turned and was about to do the same to the second when I came to my senses. I cranked the throttle on my blaster down to two, and was just about to shoot her, when Chi's blaster popped her in the butt. Bathing Beauty tumbled, face forward, over the second sleeping male.

Chi said, "I assume you wanted me to do that."

"Yeah, thanks." *Bless you, Chi.*

Evers ran forward, pulling out his medi-sensor. A few passes over the first male, and he reported, "Gone. Thoroughly dead and gone."

Bahkti, still behind me, said, "All indigenous on this planet are skilled with the knife, women and children not excepted."

Chi turned her blaster toward the side. "Seven more in the rocks," she reminded us.

I wasted a moment wondering how I was going to write this up in my report, then decided to worry about that later. I turned toward the rocks and ordered, "Fan out."

We spread out and started slowly toward the rocks, with Bahkti still behind me. Yeah, he was safer there, but he could guard my back, as well—a win for both of us.

We knew clearing these rocks wasn't going to be easy. The rocks were random and jagged, and seemed to have hundreds of hidey-holes around and under them. We had just gotten to the edges, with our blasters ready, when I heard someone behind me say "Na!"

We turned and there was Beauty, sitting on her butt, looking kind of dazed. I turned to Chi and asked, "What did you hit her with?"

Chi checked the throttle on her blaster. "Three."

And she's conscious already? Must be a tough little bird.

Beauty struggled to her feet and waved us away from the rocks. We didn't want to go in there anyway, so we followed her command. Then she turned toward the rocks and yelled, "Ya sia, ya kama, keh."

Bahkti said, "She's calling them out."

We turned to face the rocks, and sure enough, hands started to rise up out of them. As with Beauty, each hand was small and slender and female. Heads appeared between each pair of hands—heads with long, black hair and exotic, clay-brown faces. Six beautiful women stood up, three with capes, three without, all with raised hands, and all wearing bathing suits in various shades of brown or gray or dark green.

Okay, let me apologize right now for the bathing suit thing. I know they're not bathing suits, since Tashara is mostly desert, but I don't know how else to describe their clothing. A few one-pieces, the rest bikinis, I guess you could say, all of them designed to show off, as Bahkti might put it, the value of the wearer. And each of those suits was doing an admirable job of presenting its owner as being worth more alive than dead. How 'bout if I start calling them body suits. Is that better?

The six beauties stepped carefully forward until they were out of the rocks, then the Queen Beauty ordered, "Kah-nee," and each one of the six knelt in the sand and bowed her head.

Queenie looked back toward the rocks, scowled, and yelled, "Dog-fa!"

She got no response, so she yelled louder and angrier, "Dog-fa!"

Still there was no response. Queenie growled and stormed toward the rocks. She disappeared among them, then we heard a squeal, and Queenie reappeared, dragging a girl by the hair. If she had been an Earth girl, I would have put her at about ten years old, but I don't know how Tasharan women age.

This girl was dressed in rags. Queenie dragged her all the way forward, threw her face down at my feet, then she jabbed her finger at the girl and yelled at her, "Dog-shua! Pah!" and planted a foot on the girl's back.

Apparently satisfied now, she turned to the other women without taking her foot off of the girl, and ordered, "Feh da!", at which every one of them leaned forward until her forehead touched the sand. Queenie then lowered herself as well, using her left hand instead of her foot to hold down the rag girl. When Queenie lifted her head from the sand, she said something long, of which I only understood "ya panettinga."

Bahkti translated. "She says, 'May your possessions bring you wealth and pleasure.' Or, it could have been 'playthings' again, I'm still not sure."

I looked at Chi, who looked at me. I looked at Evers, who looked at me. I looked at Queenie, who looked at me. Not knowing what else to do, I said, "Keh hai"—Yes, that's fine.

///

CHI ASSERTS HERSELF

Well, I couldn't just leave them kneeling there, so I motioned them up, and since they seemed unarmed, I raised my visor. Chi and Evers and Bahkti did likewise.

Queenie introduced each one in turn. I'm terrible with names, particularly foreign ones, so I didn't really catch any of them, which was just fine with me, because I just wanted to get rid of them as soon as possible anyway. I did, though, try to listen to the name Queenie gave as her own, but it was so damn long that I just waited for her to finish so I could get Bahkti's translation. He said, "It is a difficult construct. It involves clouds and sunset and an eye of delight."

"That's too long. Got anything shorter?"

"You could call her Kah-ree. That's the 'delight' part."

"No, that won't do. What does 'queenie' mean in their language?"

"I have no idea."

I turned toward her and said, "Ya Quee Nee."

She raised her eyebrows, tilted her head from side to side, and said, "Keh. Quee Nee."

And that was that. She was now Queenie.

She pointed at me and asked, "Ya nahma?"

I answered, "Baker."

She repeated, "Beh-kur" and nodded. She seemed to like this.

I turned to Bahkti. He said, "It means 'good knowledge.'"

Well, fine.

The girl at her feet stirred. Queenie planted a foot on her again.

I asked Bahkti for the name of the girl. Bahkti asked Queenie. Queenie responded, "Dog-fa."

I turned to Bahkti for the translation. He said, "It is difficult. I'm sure it means something else in a different dialect, but it sounds like 'dog food'."

"What was the other thing she called her, 'dog shua' or something?"

Bahkti got uncomfortable, raised his hands and said, "I can't say, politely."

"Okay, we'll go with Dog-fa."

I motioned to Queenie to let the girl up. Queenie took her foot off of her and ordered, "Uff." When the girl got to her feet, Queenie grabbed her by the hair and bent her face up for my inspection. And that's when I got a surprise —the sight of a golden-eyed girl with *freckles*. Every other one of the women had black hair and soft, brown skin, but Dog-fa had russet-brown hair, somewhat lighter skin, and freckles.

I squatted to bring myself down to her height, then reached out my thumb to her face. Oops, I had to pull off my glove—then I reached my thumb to her face and brushed some of the dust from her cheek.

She looked at me like I was from another planet. Yeah,

I know, I am. But she didn't pull away. I brushed some dust from the other cheek as well, then I smiled at her. She scrunched her eyebrows, tilted her head a little, and stared at me.

"Kah-ree," I said softly.

She pulled back a little, and scrunched her chin too.

Bahkti said, "It may not mean the same thing in her tribe's language."

I stood up, figuring that was enough for now. When I took my eyes off the girl, Queenie smacked her in the face and shoved her toward the other six, who grabbed her and held her as if she might run away.

Chi said to me, "I'm getting fed up with your new bitch, boss."

"Yeah, I know. Too much of the dominance thing. But she seems to be the queen of this harem, and I need her to keep discipline among them."

Chi hesitated, then said, "Whatever you say, boss."

Yeah, I know, I was being a jerk.

At that moment, Queenie leaned toward Chi and peered into her eyes. "Si?" she asked, pointing to Chi.

Bahkti explained, "She asks if Chi is a woman."

I didn't know there was any question about that. Sure, the armor makes men and women look the same, but Chi is shorter, and her voice is higher, and I guess there's never been any question in my mind, or Evers', that Chi is a woman. But maybe it wasn't clear to a Tasharan, with an off-worlder in a suit of armor.

Meanwhile, Queenie had turned to her harem. "Si!" she said, smirking and pointing at Chi.

This pissed me off. If I was going to get my job done, I couldn't have any one of my team being dissed by the locals. And I'm sure it was pissing off Chi as well.

I turned to Chi and found her glaring at Queenie, with her jaw set tight.

Chi is one tough little fighter. She's bested me more than once in practice, because what she lacks in size she makes up for in speed and agility. Still, I could see that Queenie had a good fifteen centimeter advantage in height and a ten kilo advantage in weight, and if Chi was going to teach Queenie a lesson, she would have to do it without the advantage of her armor.

I asked her, "Chi, can you take this woman?"

Chi managed to unclench her jaw enough to answer, "Just watch me."

"Then order her to kneel. If she doesn't, you're on."

Chi called, "Hey!"

When Queenie turned to look at her, Chi beckoned her near with a sweep of her arm, pointed at the ground before her, and commanded, "Kah nee!"

Queenie stared at her for a moment, spat "Puh!", and folded her arms.

Chi held her temper. Quieter this time, she pointed to the ground before her, and said, "Kah, *nee*."

Queenie, arms still folded, shifted her weight to her other foot, stuck out the tip of her tongue, and gave Chi the raspberry. I guess some things mean the same thing in any culture.

I lifted my blaster toward Queenie just to get her attention, while Chi started to unbuckle her armor.

Queenie seemed to have no doubt as to what would come next. She simply stood there, shifted her hands to her hips, and waited, tapping her foot.

It takes a while to put on and take off our armored

suits. Queenie looked toward me, looked around as if bored, inspected her nails, winked at her harem, wiped at her nose—anything she could think of to look bored.

When Chi finally made it out of her suit, she took a step toward Queenie. The height difference was obvious. Queenie pointed at her and laughed, then turned toward her harem, held up her thumb and forefinger a centimeter apart, and said, "Ha! Wee." Her harem laughed, but nervously, I thought.

I pointed my blaster off to the side, where there was a larger patch of sand. I told Chi, "Watch for the rocks around the edges. I don't want you getting all cut up for this."

She muttered, "Thank you for your concern."

Bahkti spoke up. "Be most careful, Chi. Tasharan women practice combat from childhood."

"Thanks," she answered wryly.

When she got to the edge of the sand, Chi turned toward Queenie and yelled, "Hey! Dog shua!"

Queenie strutted slowly to the patch of sand, running her fingers through her hair and flexing her shoulder muscles. When she got there, she dropped her cloak, spat on the ground between them, and the match was on.

It took them a while to test each other's strengths and weaknesses. I've already mentioned Queenie's size advantage, and there was no denying that her muscles were fit and taut as well. Queenie, using her long limbs, landed quite a few kicks and punches on Chi. Chi was doing better with flipping her opponent.

I felt sorry for Chi. It was clear to me that she was holding back. That's *her* flaw—she doesn't have a desire to hurt an opponent. Despite her skill as a fighter, or perhaps *because* of her skill, she keeps herself in check. I've felt as much several times when I've been in the practice ring with her. I'm sure she could hurt me for real if she tried, and if I ordered her to kill Queenie I think she would, but to Chi it's about competition and exercise, not about injuring your opponent. And now it was about who's boss, not about who lives or dies.

The harem, meanwhile, was cheering every hit that Queenie put on Chi. The exception was Dog-fa—she cheered every time Queenie hit the sand. I wondered what they didn't like about each other, Queenie and the harem and Dog-fa. Was Dog-fa simply of the wrong tribe? Or was it her hair or her freckles? I just didn't know.

The match went on for too long, I thought. I needed Chi to win, but I didn't like her getting all beat up like this, so I called to her, "Another minute, Chi, and I'm calling it."

Chi took her eyes off Queenie and turned toward me, an obvious mistake, but it turned out to be intentional. Queenie, seeing her chance, jumped at Chi, who backed into her and drove her elbow up hard into Queenie's ribs. Then Chi kicked the legs out from under Queenie, dropping her on her face, and jumped on her and twisted her arm back. Chi yanked a length of string off of Queenie's body suit, wrapped it around Queenie's wrist and opposite ankle, and hog-tied her. Then she stood up, holding Queenie down with one foot, raised a fist in the air and shouted "Hey!" I'm sure that means victory in any language.

The harem stood there astonished, but Dog-fa hopped up and down and clapped her hands in delight. She ran and jumped over Queenie, then circled around the fallen leader, pointing at her and taunting, "Dog-shua, dog-shua!"

All Queenie could do was glare at her.

/ / /

HOPE

Evers pulled a regenipen out of the medikit. Regenerators are just about the coolest gadget in sports medicine in the last decade. Touch a re-gen to a wound and the bruising stops, or is reversed, all with a tingly little electric wave. Evers started on Chi's arm.

Meanwhile, I pulled a liter of water out of our supplies and handed it to her. Sure, that was a quarter of our spare water. If Chi had been wearing her suit, she wouldn't have lost so much, but fighting in this desert climate she probably lost that much or more, and I needed her to recover ASAP.

As Evers started on her other arm, I pulled Bahkti aside and motioned for Dog-fa to come over. She hesitated, but she did. I knelt again, to seem less intimidating, and gently took her by the arm.

I softened my voice. "Bahkti, ask her her name."

He did. She cast her eyes down and replied quietly, "Dog-fa."

"Bahkti, ask her what her parents named her."

He did. She glanced up at me, then down again, and whispered, "Mar-si."

Bahkti said, "Mar-si means 'ocean girl,' or 'water girl.' On a desert planet, such a name is most precious."

I lifted her chin with my index finger, looked her in the eyes, and said, "Mar-si."

Her face wrinkled and reddened and I thought for sure she was going to cry, but she held it back except for two tears, and simply nodded. I took my glove off again and wiped the tears off her dusty cheeks and smiled. Then I stood and led her to Chi, whom she hugged tight.

Evers had just about finished re-gen-ing the bruises on Chi's face. He finished up the last two and handed me the pen. Then he set about cleaning and taping Chi's cuts and scrapes.

I took the pen to Queenie, released the string which bound her wrist and ankle, and knelt beside her.

She turned over on her butt. At first she didn't want me to use the pen on her, but I pressed it to my own skin to show it was harmless, and then she let me tend to her wounds. She was surprised by the mild electric shock it delivered, but she did not object as I touched it gently to her arms, legs, and cheekbones.

I worked slowly, hoping that that it would seem more respectful to her. Her eyes alternated between watching me work and looking into my own. I started to get nervous, the way she wasn't putting up any objection. And then I looked down the length of her and hesitated.

Queenie followed my gaze and figured out what should come next—the bruise where Chi had kicked legs out. She leaned back, lifted that leg and rested it on her other knee, and smiled and batted her eyelashes at me.

Still I balked. I'd already gotten a lot more intimate with her than with any woman I hadn't been drinking with, so I just handed her the pen.

Her mouth turned down in a little pout, then she sat up and reached for the pen. She could have just taken it from me, but she reached just a little farther so that her fingers brushed mine as she took it. She was looking into my eyes as she did it, and I wondered if that extra touch meant the same thing in her culture as it would in mine.

When Evers finished taping Chi, I called Chi over and told her to bring the tape. When she got to us, I told her, right before Queenie's eyes, to tape up Queenie's cuts. I even pointed to Chi, the tape, and a couple of the cuts, so that Queenie would know what was coming.

Chi calmly said, "Sure, Boss." That's what I like about Chi. She knows what I'm thinking, and what I was thinking was that we needed to make peace between these two women. Bury the hatchet, as they used to say. Queenie must have understood it too. I don't know if in her culture enemies patch each other up, but she did not object, and watched quietly as Chi mended her.

Now that things were finally starting to calm down, I wondered why those three locals who attacked us hadn't awakened. Well, one was dead, of course, his throat slit by Queenie, but the other two should have recovered from a level 5 stun by now. I walked over to give them a kick, and was surprised to find *their* throats had been cut, too. Queenie must have done it, but when? The only times we took our eyes off of her was when she was supposedly out from Chi's zap in the butt, and when the harem was making its ways out of the rocks.

I turned to Queenie, who was watching me, and pointed at the two bodies at my feet. She shrugged her shoulders and looked at something off the other way.

I called to Bahkti. He came over to inspect the bodies. Then I asked him to ask Queenie.

She ambled over, looked at the two fresh deadsters, and said something to Bahkti.

"She says they must have killed each other."

Yeah, my ass. How was I going to write this up in my report?

Annoyed, I said to him, "This ticks me off. I wanted to get information from these guys. I wanted to know if they'd seen another off-worlder. Maybe they had seen Kozlowski."

Queenie looked at me and said, "Kozoloski?"

Had she met Kozlowski? Or does his name mean something in her language?

I turned to Bahkti. "Ask her."

She folded her arms and shrugged her shoulders, and again became mildly interested in something in the far distance.

Bahkti said, "It seems she knows something, but probably wants to be offered something for the information."

"Uh huh. Tell her we'll set her free if she leads us to Kozlowski."

Bahkti hesitated. "Um, I could do that, but I think it won't produce the results you want. You see, there is no freedom for women on this planet. If you set her free, abandon her, she would simply become the property of the next man who finds her. And what's more, setting her free would be an insult. You've earned her and the others by killing the men who owned them. Her value, along with the others, is now the equivalent of three men. If you simply set her free, it means she has no value to you. It would be like telling her that she and her friends are worthless."

"You mean I'm stuck with her?"

"Oh, no. We simply need to sell her. If you want to reward her, or at least to compliment her, you should attempt to sell her for the highest price possible."

Double shit. Buying and selling people is a court-martial offense in the Federation services.

"Ask her if she knows of anyone named Kozlowski. If she does, find out what she wants."

They had a brief exchange, during which Queenie eyed me appraisingly. Then Bahkti reported, "She wishes to know what you will give her for the information. I must explain. The people of Tashara like to bargain. You must offer her something."

Well, I'm no good at bargaining. "Tell her that if she does not lead me to Kozlowski, then she is of no use to me, and I will trade her at the next opportunity for two loaves of bread."

He turned to her and said something. She, astonished, looked at me and said, "Wah, na!"

I said, "Tell her I'm in a hurry. If she does not lead me, her price will drop to one loaf."

He said something to her again. She glared at me, pointed at herself, waved that pointing finger up and down, and declared something, I don't know what.

"She says she is insulted, that she is worth ten thousand gold palms."

I glanced down and up her. "Tell her I'm losing patience. One loaf if she does not lead me."

She must have understood, because she glared,

crossed her arms, and turned half away. She turned her head back just enough to spit the word "pah!" at me.

I turned toward Chi, who had climbed back into her suit, and to Evers, who was guarding the other women, and called, "Moving out in two." They started picking up gear, and I started toward them.

Queenie, suddenly more worried than insulted, uncrossed her arms and hurried around ahead of me. "Ik kenna, keh, ik kenna." She pointed ahead, in the direction we were headed anyway, and said, "Samarzhin. Wik ko, keh. Wik ko."

I glanced at her, but kept walking. She, walking sideways to keep up with me, pointed back to the dead locals and said something I didn't understand.

Bahkti, who was walking with me on the other side, said, "She says she will lead us to Samarzhin, but please could they strip the despicable men first. Of valuables, I think she means."

I stopped. "Okay, but make it quick."

Bahkti barely got a word out when Queenie brightened and said "Kah keh!" She turned toward the other women, smiling, and said something. She barely got two words out, when all seven of them, and Queenie too, dashed for the three bodies and rolled them like drunken sailors in an alley. I had to step in and pull a sword away from one of the women. She had her eye on a particularly nice tooled leather wristband and had started to saw off the hand that held it on.

In less than a minute the eight of them were walking away, laughing and showing off their new bracelets, anklets, earrings, and a lot of things I didn't even know what were. The three men looked like piles of empty rags.

What happened to the guns? "Wait a minute. Stop them and make them drop the weapons."

Bahkti called to them. They stopped and stared, then three of them drew long guns and pistols out from under their capes and threw them down in front of themselves.

"Swords and knives, too," I commanded.

Bahkti translated. The women glared, then three swords and four dirks appeared from under capes and under Queenie's cloak. These they threw on top of the guns.

I thought maybe I was getting the hang of this, so I commanded, "The rest of them, too."

Bahkti said something that sounded a lot like what he had said a minute ago. The women grumbled, and three shorter knives joined the stack.

I turned to Evers. "Scan them for metal."

He stepped forward, and sure enough, his scanner whistled like a tea kettle.

One by one, he scanned and pointed and more knives were surrendered. Then he came to Queenie. She spread her cloak like a bird spreads its wings to warm itself. Evers scanned one side, and she gave up something that looked like an ice pick. The other side of her cloak came up clean. Then he scanned her torso. His scanner bleeped again. He looked at me.

She looked at me too, and smirked. She just stood there with her wings spread, posing with her weight on one foot. I walked toward her, and her smile grew, and she shifted her weight to her other foot. By the time I stopped in front of her, it was clear she was planning on enjoying this.

I stepped back and called Chi over. Queenie rolled her

eyes and huffed, reached in a fold of her body suit, and pulled out a flat folding knife, which she handed to me. Then she reached behind herself and pulled out an ulu.

Evers scanned her again and she came up clean, except for the rings on the sides of her body suit.

I turned the two items over in my hands, then handed them back to her. They disappeared into her clothing in an instant.

Chi quirked an eyebrow at me as she stepped back. Yeah, we would have to watch them all the time, but I figured we would have had to anyway. I'm sure they could —or at least Queenie could—kill us with any sharp rock if we gave her a chance and if she wanted to. I figured if we didn't humiliate her any further, maybe she wouldn't want to.

/./ /

NIGHTFALL

I was in a hurry to get going, but there was the matter of the three women, plus Mar-si, who had no outer clothing. It would get down to near freezing at night, and it didn't seem fair that they should be cold. I told Bahkti to ask the women if they wanted the cloaks off the dead men's bodies. He asked, and three women and the girl scowled and spat "puh!" in unison. They crossed their arms and stood there, glaring.

Bahkti said, "We need to take these weapons with us. The indigenous would never leave them behind."

I looked toward the fallen men, then walked over and pulled the cloak off of the biggest one. Now I could see why the women didn't want the cloaks—the one I held was teeming with insects. I tossed it over a rock and jumped back and cranked my blaster to five and shot the cloak.

Carefully I walked toward it, picked it up, and shook it. Thousands of little black bodies fell to the sand, and a few maggoty looking things too. I flipped it over onto the rock and hit it with another five and shook it out again. Gosh, I hoped that was enough.

Evers and Chi wrapped the weapons in the cloak and tied it up with some utility cord, then I stood back and wondered how we were going to carry that awkward bundle.

Queenie came to our rescue with an "Ah, keh" and a few choice words to her harem. One of the women made her way into the rocks and returned with a pole about three meters long. The pole was wrapped with several strips of leather and bore metal rings that reminded me of the rings on the women's wrists, ankles, and body suits. Sure, the leather and rings would be great for lashing bundles to the pole, but I wondered if it was made for tying the women to the pole, too. Maybe the three men had been slave traders. That would explain a lot.

While I was thinking this, Queenie ordered two of the harem to tie the bundle of weapons on to the pole, then they lifted the pole onto their shoulders, turned their eyes to us, and waited for the signal to move out.

We made good time in the direction of Samarzhin. The women moved surprisingly fast. We could have kept up with them with the help of our suits, but the optimal speed in the suits is pretty much like a brisk walk. It seemed the women got frustrated with our pace, but they slowed out of respect, or perhaps they slowed so as not to appear unaccompanied.

As we walked, I asked Chi if she was okay.

"Yeah. A little sore. I'll be okay by morning."

"You think that was worth it?"

"Uh huh. I think we understand each other better now."

We followed a dry creekbed for most of the day. We knew we were on the right track because we would find a little bit of foil every kilometer or two. Then, when the sun started to near the horizon, I decided it was time to make camp.

Just off the trail we found some shallow caves that looked like they might protect us from the night's cold winds. The eight women chose the biggest cave for themselves, and the four of us chose one that gave us an easy view of the valley.

Then I had to face the problem of provisions. We had brought enough for the four of us for six days, but now we had twelve mouths to feed. I pulled an MRE out of our stock, pealed back the lid, and offered it to Queenie. She leaned forward, sniffed it, and wrinkled her nose and shook her head. I offered it to the others as well, but the few who bothered to sniff it turned up their noses.

I turned to Bahktı, who said, "Not to worry. The indigenous do not eat every day."

No wonder they're all so wiry. The image of Queenie's taught muscles, in particular, came to mind.

One of the eight hadn't come forward to inspect the meal. Mar-si now came forward, looked at the package in my hand, and looked up at me. I took the spork and scooped out some meat loaf and potatoes and stuffed it in my mouth, then handed the rest toward her. She took the spork and scooped a little bit of food and popped it in her mouth, then stuck the spork back and looked at me again. We did this until it was all gone, she and I, and the tiny corner of apple cobbler, too.

Then she went to Chi, who offered her some as well, and she went to Evers, who normally wolfs down his

MREs but for some reason had eaten particularly slowly today, and she helped him finish his. I figured maybe it had been a while since she had had solid food.

It was pretty much dark now. I took the first watch. Evers and Chi leaned back in their suits, which would maintain their temperature through the night.

The harem clustered at the back of their cave, murmuring casually among themselves, then Queenie stepped forward with two of the women. The two knelt at my feet, and Queenie said something.

I turned to Bahkti, who said, "She says, 'The value of these will not be diminished if you lie with them.'"

The value of these women? I guess I was still trying to grasp the "persons as property" thing.

I shook my head at Queenie. She seemed surprised, and waved her hand at the rest of the harem, who were watching curiously. "Ha kah-ree, na? keh?"

I shook my head again and said, "Na."

Queenie, puzzled, turned toward Evers. Indicating the two kneeling women, she asked, "Ha?" Evers shook his head.

Queenie turned to Chi and offered the two women, and waved her hand to the rest of the harem as well. "Ha?" she asked. Chi shook her head too.

Queenie helped the two up and they rejoined the others. They muttered a lot among themselves.

Bahkti said something to the women which made them nod and smile as if they understood. He turned to us and said, "I told them you were in a period of religious abstinence." Then he added, "Let me say, I think you have made the wisest choice. Women of this planet are highly resourceful. Most likely you would have been robbed blind if you had fallen asleep with any of them, and perhaps you would not have awakened at all. I urge you to be vigilant at all times."

Oh, great, I thought. *So because we said no, we might actually wake up alive tomorrow.*

It was dark now, except for the half moonlight and the little pilot lights on our armor. The seven women retreated toward the back of their cave and lay down tightly together, all in a row like spoons in a drawer. Queenie and the three who had capes cast their garments forward over the next woman so that they were all covered, and then there was quiet.

Evers and Chi lowered their visors, and Bahkti retreated to the back of our cave and lay down. That left me standing alone. I turned slightly to look out over the valley, and found Mar-si standing right there by my side. *How did she do that?*

She, in her rags, leaned slightly against me, and I guess my heart kind of broke for her. I pulled a heat pack out of the medikit and broke the seal and handed it to her and motioned for her to tuck it in her clothing. This she did, and a minute later she smiled at me, still clutching the pack under her rags.

She stood close to me for the next couple of hours, just watching out over the valley with me, until she began to teeter on her feet. I picked her up and carried her to Chi and laid her down. Chi turned on her side and draped a protective arm over the girl, all without waking up, as far as I could tell.

I returned to watch. Like I usually do when I'm alone and it's quiet like this, I thought about my ex-wife. If I hadn't opted for remote service, if I'd taken a desk job or become a trainer, we might still be together. We might have a little girl almost Mar-si's age by now. Our own little girl, innocently zooming Space Barbie around in her little pink spaceship, and maybe giving me a hug for playing with her.

My advice to anyone considering the star service is to stay home, study math, and become an accountant.

/ / /

DAY 3 - ARENA

The next day we continued to follow the trail until about noontime, when we came across the ruins of an old city. We walked through the crumbled stone walls, then on the other side of town we came across a large walled area. I led us around it to the north to sort of gauge its size which was about the size of a soccer field, then we went in by the north gate. Inside, it became clear that it was a sort of playing field or arena, with a high gate on each of the four sides.

I led us around the inside, past the west gate, to the south, where a taller structure that looked like a judges' stand provided some protection from the noonday sun. There I signaled to take a break. The women seemed relieved at this decision, and quickly lay down the pole and the bundle to sit in the shade. We four leaned against the wall, too, to give the cooling and hydration systems in our armor a chance to catch up from our morning's exertions.

We looked around. I could imagine competing teams entering by the east and west gates, where there still stood the remains of dugouts. The north gate looked like it might have been used to herd in animals. The walls all around were a little over two meters high, and seemed to have a tiered top for standing or sitting spectators.

I looked at the women sitting there chatting, and dug in our supplies and pulled out another liter of water. Yeah, that meant we would be down to half. We hadn't planned on another eight mouths to provide for, but I couldn't let them just dehydrate. I twisted open the bottle and handed it to Queenie, who looked through it at her women and smiled. Then she took a drink, and another one, and passed the bottle. Each of the other six women looked through it, too, to see the others distorted by the round bottle, and took a couple of swigs. Then they handed it back to me.

I took the bottle. It wasn't even half empty yet. But they had forgotten one of them. I handed the bottle to Mar-si, and she looked up to me gratefully and took two drinks and handed it back to me. As I capped the bottle, I looked at the seven women. None of them seemed happy that Mar-si had gotten a drink, too.

I offered the bottle to them again, but they shook their heads no. Was that all they wanted? If so, they were remarkably adapted to desert life. There was another possibility, which was that they wouldn't drink from it after Mar-si did. Just in case they were thinking that, I unscrewed the cap again and took a drink just to show them it was okay.

I walked back to Evers and Chi and Bahkti. They seemed to be pretty much at ease. I said, "I want to check the mood of these women, to see if they're reliable. Chi, you take a walk out the west gate, and Bahkti, you wander out the north gate. I'll go out here and make my way around to the east. Set your blasters on stun three or something. Evers, you watch the women, but not too close. Set your blaster on low. I want to see if they try anything. If nothing happens in half an hour, just come on back. Okay?"

They shrugged and said, "Okay, boss."

Bahkti and Chi, one after another, wandered off and disappeared out their gates. I stretched my arms, called Mar-si over, pointed to the south gate, and we started to walk out. That left Evers alone. From just outside the south gate, I saw him sit down in the shade to relax.

I knelt in front of Mar-si and raised a finger to my lips in a gesture I hoped she would understand, and she did likewise and nodded. Then I led her eastward a ways until we were pretty much near the women, but on the other side of the wall, and there I stopped to listen. I could hear that their conversation, which had just been low chatter, change to occasional, short sentences. It sounded to me like they were planning something. Mar-si looked at me, kind of concerned.

We listened hard as their talk quieted to excited whispers, and then there was a clear, high "yoo hoo," and the sound of feet running off to the east. I started to the east, too, and I heard Evers' blaster go off at its lowest setting. The women's voices were back now, sounding excited.

Mar-si and I listened and looked up, trying to gauge where they were. It seemed they were near the east gate. And then I heard Queenie's voice, loud and clear and right above us on the wall. She was calling "Heh, mahna, mahna, yoo hoo, yoo hoo," in the most mocking voice I'd heard since middle school, and then I heard a blaster fire at kill one.

The beam shot into the sky, right over the east gate. I heard Queenie call, "Woo hoo!", and then I saw her jump off the wall, right above me. She was grinning to put the sun to shame, right up until she landed in my arms, at which point she gawked at me, totally astonished. A half second later she squirmed and launched herself out of my arms and hit the ground running.

I shot her in the back of the knees with a stun one, and she crumpled to the sand. She tried to get up, but her legs wouldn't hold. Believe me, I know exactly how that feels from field practice at the academy.

I got to hand it to her, though, she was tough. She didn't give up. Half-lying on the ground, she turned to me and glared, then got her legs underneath herself and struggled to her feet. She took a few steps away, and it looked like she was going to make it, so I glanced another stun one her way, which sent her sprawling.

Mar-si ran up to her, looking awfully concerned, and I walked up to her too. Queenie turned herself enough to look up at me again and glare. "Ya gurun mahna, keh," she mocked, but there wasn't much she could do about it— she just held herself up as best she could, breathing hard. Mar-si reached out to her in a concerned sort of way, but Queenie scowled and slapped her hand away.

Mar-si and I just waited as she caught her breath, then Queenie managed to roll over until she was sitting on her butt. She glared at me again, a sort of mixture of anger and embarrassment, I guessed.

Okay, maybe I was too hard on her. I holstered the blaster and knelt and scooped an arm under hers and another under her knees. She rolled a little toward me and put an arm around my neck, and then she let me lift her up. I turned and headed back toward the south gate, with Mar-si following.

It wasn't a long walk, just a little over sixty meters. I looked at Queenie to see how she was doing, and found her studying me. Well that felt weird, mainly because I couldn't gauge her expression, but I could tell it wasn't anger and it wasn't pain. And then she did something I wasn't expecting, which was to roll toward me in my arms and turn her head and lean in around the jaw bar of my helmet, and she kissed me.

I stopped, dumbfounded. She tilted her head back to look into my eyes, and then leaned in for another kiss.

She adjusted her position in my arms a little for a better angle, and she kissed me again, as hard as my gear would allow. Her lips, which had felt dry the first time, now felt full and warm and moist, and became moister as she kept on kissing me.

Man alive, she felt good. I could have given in right there, if it hadn't occurred to me that she would bite me and jump out of my arms and run again, but she didn't, she just let the kissing run its course, and she finished up by running the tip of her tongue around my lips for good measure. Then she leaned back just enough to look me in the eyes and grin, and then she waited to see what I would do.

I set her on her feet, which seemed to hold her up quite well now. She had one arm around me still, holding herself to me. With her other hand she reached to the side of her body suit and pulled the knot loose, and she tugged at the lacings to loosen them. Then she ran her hand up the side of my suit and popped open one of the fasteners.

39

With both hands I moved her to arm's length. She held my eyes as she loosened more of her lacing, then she pointed to the sandy ground at our feet and asked, "hee?"

I couldn't believe it! I must have been misinterpreting something, because it seemed like she was offering herself to me, right here, with Mar-si standing just an arm's length away. She just kept on unlacing, waiting for my answer.

Finally I got a grip and shook my head and waved my hands in a "no" motion and said "na, na," to boot.

She stopped unlacing. I pointed to Mar-si and covered her eyes, hoping to show that what she was suggesting was inappropriate. Queenie scowled at Mar-si and spat the word "pah" at her, then Queenie turned away and started lacing back up again.

I felt Mar-si tugging at my arm. I looked down at her and she pointed at Queenie and said, "Ya, si, keh," and then she covered her own eyes with one hand. I shook my head again, and said, "Na, na." She looked into my eyes with her brow scrunched like she didn't understand, and took a step back.

Queenie finished tying the knot at her hip. Without looking at me, she shook her mane, ran her fingers through it, took a deep breath and squared her shoulders, then she marched toward the south gate. Mar-si and I followed. As best as I can remember, this was the first time I've ever tried to walk in armor while I had a hard-on.

Inside the gate, Queenie turned to the right toward her harem, who rushed forward to welcome her back. I turned left to where Evers and Bahkti and Chi were waiting.

Evers spoke first. "I hope you don't mind I shot at her, boss. She was up over the gate, just out of stun range, waving her butt at me and taunting me. I thought a little ear warmer would be appropriate."

"Yeah, sounds about right. I'm sure she had it coming."

Chi, her arms crossed in front of her, was eyeing me critically. Now she said, "You get what you wanted out of that little exercise, boss?"

I answered, "Yeah, I think we understand each other better now."

Most of the time it's really reassuring that Chi knows what I'm thinking. This was not one of those times.

/ / /

WOLVES

We made good progress that afternoon. And as before, as the sun neared the western horizon, I began to look for a place to shelter for the night. We climbed the slope of the valley and found some some shallow caves along the cliff face. The women set down the pole with the bundle of weapons.

There was an open area in front of the caves. I wished the boulders were closer, to block anyone from seeing us, but it was getting too late to find a better site.

The setting sun turned the western sky a bright red. I took a few minutes to watch the glow spread. Chi and Evers and Bahkti joined me. Queenie walked over, too, and looked west, then she looked at us. I think she was wondering what was so interesting out there. And then we heard a coyote howl.

Queenie stiffened and turned westward toward the sound.

"Uh, oh," said Bahkti, turning west also.

"What?" I asked. And then we heard an answering howl.

"Gurun kanora," he answered. Queenie echoed,

"Gurun kanora."

She took a few steps forward and scanned the valley westward, from whence we had come. The valley was rapidly becoming a sea of long shadows cast by the setting sun. Then she turned and hurried toward the harem. They were clustered around the bundle of weapons, watching anxiously and whispering among themselves. She pointed to the bundle. "Keh shneh, shneh." They tore into the bundle.

Bahkti explained. "Gurun kanora are like wolves. They hunt in packs." He lifted his blaster to check the charge. Evers and Chi and I reflexively did the same.

"Are they dangerous?" I asked, immediately realizing it was the stupidest question I'd ever asked.

"Think wild boars or brown bears in terms of size, and a dozen coming at you at once."

Another howl blew toward us on the wind, followed by two answering howls.

Bahkti added, "Those three bodies we left behind? They are no more."

I looked back toward the women. Every one of them had a weapon in each hand, and each one of them was trying to make her way to the back of the cave, but the cave wasn't deep enough.

Evers and Chi lifted their sensors. "Static," he reported. "No, wait ... life forms at 400 meters. Half a dozen, maybe more. They must be big, to register above the background noise."

Suddenly the boulders seemed too close, rather than too far away. If there were half a dozen bear-sized wolves coming, I'd rather have had a longer field of fire.

"Evers, Chi, set to kill one. Bahkti, you and I will do

stun eight, wide angle." We cranked the throttles on our weapons. With these settings, I hoped that Bahkti and I could keep them at bay while Evers and Chi terminated them.

The light was going fast. I heard voices raised behind me, and turned to see the women pushing Mar-si out of the cave. She ran around to the other side and tried to force her way in, but two women grabbed her by the arms and threw her out. "Kanora fa," they said, their voices sounding kind of panicky.

Mar-si was panicking even more, and she was crying. She ran at the middle of the harem, couching down and trying to get between their legs. Four of them grabbed her by the arms and legs, carried her a few steps out, and threw her as far as they could. "Ya fa," they shouted. "Ya kanora fa!"

She picked herself up. She was sobbing and her face was crimson and streaked with tears. She looked for an opening between them, but they held up their swords and knives and waved her away, shouting, "Ya fa!"

I grabbed Mar-si and pulled her behind me. I could feel my jaw tightening as I leveled my blaster at them. I cranked my blaster to five, the most I could justify with someone who wasn't trying to kill me. But they were trying to kill Mar-si, or at least to feed her to the wolves.

Chi appeared at my side, her blaster leveled at them too. She slowly turned her throttle ring to mid-way as well.

Evers called, "A dozen of them at 200 meters."

I raised my blaster. I could feel my hands starting to shake in anger. I worried about my trigger finger—it seemed to want to pull, without me even commanding it.

Queenie must have sensed how close they were to getting shot. She stepped forward in front of her terrified flock, faced me, and crossed her arms, all the while holding a sword in one hand and a knife in the other. She looked me straight in the eyes, and her jaw was set.

I recognized the fear and determination on her face. I'd seen it before, on Chi and Lance Corporal Parker just before their first real firefight. That incident is burned into my memory because Parker and two others didn't survive. And now Chi was here beside me, her jaw set like mine and Queenie's.

But Chi must have been cooler than I was, because she could verbalize. She said, "They need to be taught a lesson, boss, but now is not the time."

Evers called, "Twenty, at 100 meters. They're big, boss. Mind if I bump it up to kill 2?"

That pulled my attention away from the harem. Sure enough, the baying was coming closer, and I could hear excited yipping, too.

I called to Evers, "Crank it to whatever you need, just know you'll need to take our your half of the twenty."

He answered, "It's two dozen, at 50 meters."

I stepped around Mar-si and took my position on the right. Chi filled in between Evers and me. I called to him, "Evers, cover Bahkti. His armor's lighter."

"Copy, boss."

I silently cursed the boulders, only fifteen meters away, which would hide the attackers. If we only had a longer field of fire ...

We could hear the eager growls of the pack. Evers called, "Thirty of them at 20 meters. All sizes."

In between the rocks I could see eyes glinting in the

46

moonlight.

"Visors," I called. "Forward lights. FPF.*"

* Final Protective Fire

Wolves the size of mastiffs burst from between the boulders. The night lit up with blaster fire.

They warned us at the academy that adrenaline blocks out rational thought. That's why they train us—so that we can act out of instinct when things get really hairy. And that night, things literally got hairy. Beasts the size of rhinos and as small as rottweilers charged us. Bodies began to stack up, whether stunned or dead. They kept coming, climbing over and around their fallen packmates, scurrying and jumping and falling on us from every side. In the flashes of blaster fire I saw Queenie on my right, sword slashing and knife stabbing. To my left I saw Mar-si, crouching beside Chi, stabbing a kanora with her long knife. And I could hear recharge signals whistling from several blasters, including my own.

At last the fury died down, and then there was silence, except for the beep-beep-beep of low charge warnings. I swept my light from side to side, as did Bahkti and Evers and Chi. One wolf crawled out from under another and tried to run for the rocks. I heard Chi's trigger click and click again, and then her gun fired and the wolf fell, and her charge alarm sounded again. Mar-si ran forward and stabbed it behind its jaw.

I called for a sensor check. Evers reported, "Nothing closer than 50." Chi reported, "Nothing closer than 60." Evers added, "Ditto."

I lifted my visor, and the smell of burning flesh hit my

nostrils, making me gag. Where was the wind when you needed it?

I looked around us. Queenie picked up a dog-sized kanora by the fur, carried it to the edge of the kill zone, and threw it over a rock. Over near Bahkti, I saw two women stab another kanora, then they dragged it out toward the rocks. Then the women regrouped in the cave, and stared at us.

I looked at them, then looked at my team. They all seemed as exhausted as I was.

Queenie walked out from among the women, carrying her sword in one hand and a knife in the other. She walked past me, then along the pile of dead bodies, and then she climbed over the heap and up onto one of the taller boulders. She raised her sword and her knife and yelled out a long, alternating, two-pitch cry, sounding very much like a siren. When it ended, I heard it echo off the opposite canyon wall, and again off of another rock wall farther down the valley.

The other seven women, Mar-si included, rushed out of the cave and climbed over the beasts and onto the boulders, and all eight repeated Queenie's cry in unison. Again the canyon resounded with their call.

Chi, standing next to me, said, "The same goes for me, boss."

"Ditto that, Chi."

The women climbed down and made their way back to the cave, smiling and laughing and hugging each other, all except Mar-si, who ran to Chi and threw her arms around her.

Well, fine.

I knew I wouldn't be able to go to sleep anyway, so I claimed first watch. Chi said she would, too. Bahkti told us to go ahead, he needed some sleep, and Evers dittoed that.

The night fell quiet, except for the click and chirp of insects. A cool wind picked up just enough to blow some of the stench away. I climbed a boulder now, too, and Chi joined me. We just stared out into the eerie, moonlit darkness, seeing nothing moving, just as it should be. Then Mar-si climbed up in between us, and put an arm around Chi and an arm around me.

/ / /

DAY 4 - PROMONTORY

The next morning I woke up with a start. Evers must have let me sleep late, because the sun was well up over the horizon. The women were bustling about.

Seeing me sit up, Evers said, "They've been up since dawn, carving up the carcasses. Eyeballs seem to be highly prized, and tongues, too, and something else I won't mention, if you know what I mean."

I could guess, but didn't want to think about it, let alone voice it.

I walked out among the rocks. In a smaller clearing, I saw two women working with knives, peeling the hide off of a medium-sized kanora. On the way back to the main clearing, I saw several things that must have been tongues drying on top of rocks, and a couple dozen eyeballs, and eight or ten things I'd rather not describe.

Back near the cave, I saw the black cloak lying on the ground, the useless guns still resting in it, and the swords lying on top. None of the knives were there. I figured they were all in use. I didn't know if they would make it back to the cloak without the aid of scanners. The women had wielded them so bravely last night, and hadn't made a single aggressive move toward us since we stripped them of them, so I figured I wouldn't press the issue.

Next to the black cloak, two hides lay drying in the sun. Women were poking holes in the edge, while others were cutting kanora intestines into long strips.

They seemed to need more time for their projects, so I walked over to our supply pack and pulled out a multi-tool. It took me half an hour of hard work to saw two ten-centimeter canines out of a medium-sized kanora, then it was Evers' turn to use the tool.

I motioned Bahkti over, and caught up with Queenie, who was making the rounds of her harem.

"Ask her when her people will be ready to go."

He asked her something. She looked at me as if the question made no sense. Then, with palms upraised, she answered to Bahkti. Bahkti said, "She says, we are ready at your command."

"Okay," I said. "Fifteen minutes."

Bahkti said something to her, and she started barking orders to her troops. The women gathered up their spoils of war, wrapped them in the hides, wrapped up the guns and swords, and fastened the bundles onto the long pole. When I gave the signal to move out, three of them hefted the pole onto their shoulders and off we went.

I should have said, probably, that since we left that abandoned town, we'd been walking on a sort of road headed eastward. It didn't take a genius to figure it led to Samarzhin, and it worried me, because sooner or later we were bound to meet some locals on this road, and I didn't want them running ahead of us alerting the authorities that there was a company of off-worlders on their way. I asked Bahkti to ask Queenie how far, and the answer came back "tomorrow." So out of caution I sent Bahkti and Evers ahead to scout out the way. They would warn us if we were going to encounter anyone, in which case we would hide.

By late afternoon, Evers radioed back that they could see a city in the distance, and that there wasn't any cover along the road. There was no way a dozen of us could make it to the city unobserved. I looked around and saw a promontory off to our left, a good ways away from the road. It looked like a good spot from which to plan our next step, so I radioed back that we would meet them there.

We left the women in the rocks below the promontory. The four of us started up what you could call a goat path along the side of the cliff, except I couldn't imagine there were any goats out here in the desert. Queenie followed us, for some reason. Then we made our way to the edge of the cliff overlooking the city, and there we sat down.

I didn't think it would work to just walk into town tomorrow and say, "Take us to your Kozlowski," so what we decided on was that Bahkti would slip in to town tonight, scope out the situation, and meet us back here tomorrow night. None of us liked the idea of him going in alone, but that's his particular skill. It's what he's trained for, and what he's paid for. Shooting gurun kanora? That's just a sideline.

We made our way back down to camp, where it was already well into twilight. We debated whether to let Bahkti wear his endosuit into the city. I made the call that he would wear it. Sure it would mark him as an off-worlder if it was discovered, but I figured it would also mark him as someone special, rather than some run-of-the-mill spy, and maybe he would get special treatment. We unwrapped the black cloak and draped it over him to help hide the endosuit and to give him more cover in the darkness.

Queenie had been watching us all this time. I don't know how much of our conversation she understood, but when she saw us drape the cloak over Bahkti, she became really agitated. She stepped up and waved her hands and said, "na, na," and she made a slashing motion across her neck and made a sound that sounded like "k-x-x-x-t." Then she said something to Bahkti.

Bahkti turned to us and said, "She says if I wear this cloak into the city, they will kill me."

Queenie reached for the clasp of her cloak and undid it and held her cloak out to Bahkti. He undid his black cloak and tried to hand it to her, but she wouldn't touch it, she just pushed her cloak toward him. He handed the black cloak to Chi and took Queenie's dark green cloak and draped it over his shoulders. Queenie stepped forward to fasten the clasp, then stepped back to appraise him, and grudgingly nodded her head.

Well, it was time to let him go. I told him if he didn't come back, I would write up a glowing commendation for his personnel file. He thanked me and said he would think of me as he was being tortured. And with that, he set off with Evers, who would accompany him as far as he thought was safe.

/ / /

DAY 5 - WAITING

The next day passed slowly. The women laid out their booty to dry in the sun, and staked out the hides as well. Along with the tongues and eyeballs and other things, they had brought along several forelegs, which they now proceeded to strip down to the bones. They took special care with the tendons, which I imagined they would use for tying up something or other. They also spent a good amount of time cleaning the bones, then they set them out to dry.

By mid-day they seemed pretty bored. A few of them napped, while the others collected handfuls of pebbles, dug a series of tiny depressions in the hard earth, and started to play a game that looked like mancala.

By late afternoon they were getting antsy. Queenie came up to me and said something I didn't understand, then she said the same thing more slowly, and with gestures. The message included pointing to her stomach and to her mouth, where she made forking-in motions, and pointing out toward the distance. I guessed she wanted to go get food, so I nodded and said, "keh."

She gathered her flock, Mar-si included, and they set

off. I sent Chi after them because it seemed like we should be keeping an eye on them.

Half an hour later they were back, carrying a half dozen tuber kind of things that looked like oblong coconuts, or hairy, extra-long potatoes. Chi said they had dug them out of the ground.

They proceeded to hold them up to the sky as if they were thankful, then they cracked them open on the edges of some rocks. They scraped out the insides with their knives, which produced heaps of fiber that looked like spaghetti squash. This they shared among themselves.

Queenie brought one of these tubers to me, already cracked and scraped. "Fa," she said, and she showed how to eat it, which was pretty much just put the fiber in your mouth and chew it. I followed her lead. It tasted kind of bland, like a potato, but I nodded and said "hai," which I hope meant "good."

I opened the third liter of water and offered it to Queenie. She took a couple of swigs again, and passed it around. The others drank and played with looking through the clear bottle again, to see how it distorted things, and when it came back to me, it was still half full. I don't know how they could survive on so little food and water.

Sunset came quickly here under the cliff. The seven women gathered in a circle, knelt together, and laced their arms around each other's shoulders. With their heads touching in the center, one began to sing in a low, slow voice. The others joined in. I had no idea what the song was about, but it sounded kind of mournful. I glanced over at Chi, and found her watching the group intently. I wondered if she understood what they were singing, or maybe she just understood the mood of it.

Us guys in the star service are generally loners. We have to be, because we can't keep up relationships strung out over the years and across the light-years. I guess I'd assumed that Chi was like us, that relationships weren't important, or at least that she'd given up on them, but now I started to wonder.

The women rose and embraced each other, then made their way to their chosen shelter. Queenie, who on other nights had anchored one end of the line, this time took second position, with another woman's cape spread over her. They pulled a couple of the newly-dried hides over themselves, too.

Seven of them. Where was Mar-si? I looked around and found her leaning against Chi. They were watching the women. Chi and Mar-si had each wrapped an arm around the other.

Bahkti returned in the small hours of the morning. Evers had been standing watch and brought him in. Chi and I woke at the sound of their whispers. He was excited to report that the big news from a few days ago was that there was an off-worlder imprisoned in the palace. It was rumored that he was wild and uncouth, and that a whole squad of guards was needed to keep him subdued. This didn't sound anything like Kozlowski, but I hoped there was enough truth in it to confirm that he was still alive.

Bahkti hadn't slept in nearly two days, so we agreed we'd go over the situation in the morning, and then work out a plan.

/ / /

DAY 6 - CAPTURE

After daybreak we got Bahkti's full report. Apparently it was just your typical pre-medieval city, with a surrounding wall and guarded gates and a shanty town outside the wall. There was a broad street leading from the main gate toward a fortress-like palace, and there were at least three other, smaller gates, one of which led out to the waste dump.

"How'd you get in," I asked.

"Just followed some other guys in. They seemed to be scrap dealers or something. The guards searched their wagon. For some reason they didn't search me. I guess the cloak worked."

At that moment he looked up and realized Queenie was standing nearby, listening. He took off the cloak and handed it to her and said, "Tak hai, keh." She took it and answered, "Hai, keh."

"What about the palace?"

"Built like a fortress around an inner courtyard. No windows on the lower level, narrow windows in the upper part of the wall. Main gate well guarded, rear gate closed and barred most of the time, and it seems to be guarded as well. I didn't get inside."

We kicked around some ideas for how to enter the city, trick our way into the palace, and so forth. I must admit my go-to strategy is to walk softly and carry a big stick. Bahkti, however, pointed out that Commander Phillips' mission was to find tribes we can work with, and breaking into palaces with loaded weapons might complicate that.

At this point, Queenie, who had been watching us intently, stepped forward and talked to Bahkti. She asked a question that involved pointing to us and the city and the word "Kozoloski." He confirmed whatever she asked. She asked another question that involved herself, the harem, and the city. Bahkti said, "She asks, why don't we just trade the eight of them for Kozlowski."

Well, I must admit it sounded simple, but, "Tell her there are four of us, and the king has many armed men. We don't want to get into a fight with them."

Queenie said something that involved pointing to me, to my blaster, to herself, to my team, to the women, and the city.

Bahkti translated. "She says to take her and the others into the city as hostages. Point our weapons at them, meaning the women. She says the people of the city will not attack us, lest we damage our property, which they could not then purchase from us."

"You mean we would be safe because they want to buy our women?"

"Or trade for them. I must say, ownership of women and other slaves is comparatively sacrosanct. They would rather acquire such property fair and square, rather than steal them."

"And after we've sold them, or traded them?"

"Well, I think that would be a different situation then, and at that point we would have to be highly vigilant."

I looked at Queenie, who seemed to be waiting patiently, and I looked at my team. Evers said, "If we play our cards right, we would have Kozlowski by then, and it would just be a matter of working our way out of the city."

I scratched my head, or would have, if my helmet hadn't been in the way. Instead, the best I could do was wiggle my helmet over my crew cut.

I surveyed my team. Their answers were, "Sounds like a plan," "Potential for peaceful resolution," and "Whatever you say, boss."

I looked over to the women. They seemed to be pretty much waiting for us to make up our minds, so I said, "We move in fifteen minutes."

Queenie barked something at her harem, and they got busy packing up their stuff.

Two of them climbed a couple meters up the cliff, dug at a thin rock layer, and came back with orangey-red clay. This they further crushed, then they spat on it and mixed it and smeared it on their faces. The seven then helped each other blend and feather this coloring to highlight their cheekbones. One of the gatherers glanced at Mar-si, who was watching them, and smeared a couple of streaks onto her cheeks. Chi took off her gloves and helped her blend it in, then smiled at her, and Mar-si smiled back.

By fifteen minutes they were waiting beside their carrying pole, ready to go. Queenie came up to me. We already had our blasters in our hands. She lifted mine, rested it against her abdomen, turned the throttle all the way down, and then bumped it up one. Then, still holding the blaster, she turned around and, looking at me over her shoulder, poked the muzzle of it into the small of her back. "Keh?" she asked.

"Keh," I answered. She nodded, and pointed at my team to do likewise with the harem. Then she flipped her hood over her hair, and I gave the order to move out.

We attracted quite a bit of attention as we approached the city gates—an assortment of men, women and children began to trail us and to walk along side us, though at a safe distance.

When we got within ten meters of the main gate, five burly men carrying battle blades came out and barred our path. A squad of ten lesser armed men followed them out, with half splitting on each side of us, keeping about five meters away. Burly Number Three waved his battle blade at us, and commanded something.

We stopped, with Queenie out in front, me immediately behind her, the harem behind me, and my team behind them.

Burly Number Three said something to Burly Number Five, who stepped forward in front of Queenie. He pushed back the hood of her cloak.

His eyes popped and his jaw dropped. He stepped back, and the other four burlies went goggle-eyed too. The crowd in the background gasped.

"Da!" commanded Queenie sharply. The five burlies dropped to one knee, still staring at her.

Queenie looked left and right at the dumbfounded squad. "Da, ya shua-a!" she barked at them. All ten of them dropped to their knees and bowed their heads.

"Ya!" she called to Burly Number Three. She followed

this with a long command I didn't understand. He got up, smacked burlies two and four out of the way, and bade her follow him. I poked my blaster into her back just for show, and that, my friend, is how we got escorted into the city.

A minute's walk got us to the palace. Burly Three was hollering orders ahead of us as we approached the palace gate, which was dutifully opened for us. Burly Three stepped aside and bowed. I followed Queenie in, my blaster still pointed at the small of her back. The eight women followed me, and my team followed them, blasters still pointed. Bahkti then made his way to my side.

An officious-looking man rushed forward to question Queenie, but she just waved him away. She walked right into an inner court and up to an empty throne waiting in the shade at the far end, where she stopped. Then she yelled something really loud at the walls and ceiling.

Two officials and two menial servants appeared, then a large man in an ornate robe. As the man made his way to the throne, I couldn't help but stare at the gold-work trimmings on his dark green robe. You know with our technology, cranking out yards of gold-colored ribbon is no challenge whatsoever, but with the primitive technology of this planet, I realized that this man's robe must have been hand-embroidered in this intricate design using actual fine gold thread. I must say I was thoroughly impressed.

The man stopped in front of the throne and glared at Queenie. Queenie dropped to one knee and bowed her head, which seemed to mollify the old man somewhat. The harem knelt, too.

He started speaking to her in a low, rumbly voice, and

did not stop. His voice rose in volume as he continued, and he gestured toward her quite a bit, until he was practically shouting. His gestures became more effusive, and he ended by pointing at me and my team and then he jabbed his finger toward her and shouted some final words, which echoed throughout the court.

Queenie, head still bowed, turned a little toward me and Bahkti and said something brief. Bahkti translated. "She says her father requests that we lower our weapons." Queenie added something else, and Bahkti said, "She says it is safe to do so."

I took my blaster off of her, cradled it in my left arm, and took my hand off the handle and trigger. Bahkti and Evers and Chi did likewise. I showed him my empty right palm.

Her father lowered himself onto his throne and told her something with the word "uff" in it, which I remembered from our first encounter with Queenie. She rose, bowed deeply to him, then beckoned to her harem to bring the pole of booty forward. As they untied the black bundle, she explained something to him that involved pointing to me.

Two of the harem laid the black bundle at his feet and untied it, bowing as they did so. He gestured and spoke. They pulled at the black cloak, unceremoniously dumping the guns and swords on the stone floor, and brought the cloak to him. He inspected it closely, then nodded appreciatively and asked me something.

Bahkti translated. "He asks if you really destroyed three of the black-cloaked vermin."

Queenie answered something that began with "keh." The answer included the slashing motion across her throat and the sound "k-x-x-x-x-t" and ended with "gurun kanora fa." The king eyed me appraisingly and asked, "Uh?"

Bahkti said, "She confirmed that you completely humbled them, cut their throats, and left them for kanora food."

The king beamed and rose from his throne, and descended the steps to our level. "Eh hai! Eh hai!" he declared, and then he slapped me on the back several times.

He turned to his daughter and said something that I didn't understand at all—the vowels and consonants didn't match anything I had heard so far. I glanced at Bahkti and he seemed to be confused too, or maybe he was just listening very intently.

The king's words ended with a question, and he pointed to me. Queenie bowed her head and shook it no. He paused to consider this, then asked her a shorter question. Again she shook her head no. He seemed relieved. He nodded and said something very brief, the tone of which made me think he probably said "good."

Whatever he had been discussing with his daughter must have been resolved to his satisfaction, because he straightened up and his smile returned..

He motioned to his courtiers and said something that included pointing at all of us in a grand gesture, then he departed toward whence he came, laughing and patting his prodigious stomach.

Bahkti explained, "We are invited to dinner this evening. In the meantime, we are to be guided to our accommodations."

A courtier and a menial bowed and beckoned us

toward one of the archways. Our harem—which I had come to think of as our security—did not accompany us.

As we followed the menial, I nudged Bahkti. "What were they saying?"

He whispered to me, "I don't know. They were speaking in their family language, which is used when they don't want to be understood. But my guess is, he was asking her if you made her yours."

So I asked, "What do you mean? I thought she declared herself, and the other women, as my possessions."

"Well, there is possession, and there is ownership, and their is making something yours. ..."

Now I was puzzled, and I'm sure it showed.

Still following the menial, we began to ascend a flight of stairs. Bahkti continued, "Suppose you buy a blaster, and you intend to resell it. You possess it, but you don't intend to make it yours. Or you could buy a blaster, test fire it just to see how it performs, and then sell it."

"Yeah, people do that all the time."

Bahkti nodded. "But suppose you like the way it performs, like the way it handles, and you decide to keep it for yourself. You holster it and carry it on your hip, you keep it ready for when you need it, and you come to depend on its presence. You've 'made it yours,' so to speak."

"Ah, ..." I nodded. "... and I have not made her mine."

He glanced at me. "That is my impression."

We turned a corner. My thoughts went back to my encounter with Queenie outside the arena walls. No, I hadn't "made her mine." I hadn't even "test fired" her, other than at stun one. And considering a father's point of view, it was probably a good thing I hadn't.

The menial guided us through a large door and into a long hallway. He opened the doors along one side and said something which I'm sure meant that these rooms were for us, then he backed out, bowing as he went. He exited by the door we had entered from. We saw the door close, and we heard a bar thrown, and I got the distinct feeling we were prisoners. We were still wearing our gear, and we were still fully armed, but we were prisoners nonetheless.

A side door opened at the end of the hall, and a head popped out, then the entire owner stepped out into the hallway. He blinked at us and said, "Baker, is that you?"

"Koz?"

He rushed down the hallway, beaming, and threw his arms around me and we clapped each other on the back, and then he pulled away and shook hands with Chi and Evers and threw his arms around Bahkti and they hugged each other and shook hands like long-lost pals.

/ / /

BANQUET

Late in the afternoon, two women entered by a door at the other end of the hallway. They brought pitchers of water and towels and said something to Koz, who explained that we were invited to dine with the king, and would we please clean ourselves up. He smiled at them and answered for us. I noticed that one of the women smiled a little more shyly at him than the other, and I think she kind of blushed, too.

I didn't want to leave our armor unattended, so we wore it to dinner. Our blasters can be hung on the back of our suits, so at least we didn't look like we were itching to shoot up the place. An extra-large guard stood at each side of the throne. Each held a battle-axe and looked like he was ready to use it. I felt conscious that our armor was particularly vulnerable at the neck, so I whispered to my team that we should behave ourselves and not make any sudden moves.

Koz whispered that we should stand and wait, so we did. I scanned the room, then took a good look at the square table before us. it was loaded from edge to edge with every kind of food I could imagine, and as much more that I couldn't have imagined. I tell you, after a week of MREs, I was just about ready to dive into this table like it was a swimming pool.

After a respectful delay, Queenie walked in, stood next to the throne, and winked at me. There followed another respectful delay, during which Queenie rocked on her heels and rolled her eyes. Then a courtier appeared and announced something in a loud and ceremonious voice. He gestured toward the archway and bowed his head. Queenie turned toward the archway and bowed her head too, so we all did, and then the king appeared, once again introduced by the courtier. He walked to his throne, cleared his throat, sat down, and gestured for us to sit.

I won't bore you with the details of the banquet. I will say, though, that the same serving girl who blushed so demurely earlier that afternoon was serving my side of the table, with Bahkti and Koz and me. She was quick to fill our water cups and wine goblets and to hand us anything we reached for. Outside of this obvious efficiency, I noticed that she preferred to stand immediately behind Koz, and I'm sure I saw him "accidentally" brush her ankle more than once.

There was a point, though, at which the king must have asked for a report of Queenie's adventures, because she rose to her feet and started narrating and acting out our encounter with the gurun kanora. She gnashed her teeth and made biting motions with her hands, and sweeping gestures as the kanora attacked in waves. Her imitation of blasters involved the sound effect "bee, bee, bee," and her own part in the adventure involved a lot of slashing and stabbing. She wrapped up the story by walking slowly around the table and patting Evers and Chi and me and Bahkti on the back, during which she spoke with awe about our heroics.

She ended the story by reaching for a plate of something that looked like sugar-coated eggs. She knelt and offered this to me and bowed her head. I took one of the eggs and looked at it. I assumed I was supposed to eat it.

She took one as well, and handed the plate to Bahkti. Then, still kneeling, she brought it to her mouth and bit into it. She mmmm'd in ecstasy as golden jelly oozed from it, then she licked her lips where it had begun to escape her mouth. She looked me in the eyes and beamed.

Bahkti said, "I think you'd best eat it, Boss."

"What is it," I asked, biting into it as she had done. The golden jelly didn't taste like egg yolk.

"Kanora eyes," he responded.

I clamped my teeth shut so as not to spew this delicacy onto the woman who had so generously offered it. I forced the corners of my mouth up into a smile.

Delighted, she asked, "Hai, keh?" and took another bite of her kanora eyeball. "Mmmm," she repeated, her eyes closing in delight.

I nodded, the smile still glued to my mouth. I tried to gather my courage for the duty of swallowing.

We ate as much as we thought we safely could. Chi and Baker seemed as cautious as I was. Bahkti and Koz enjoyed tasting a little bit of everything. When our host seemed to have eaten his fill, he motioned for the serving girls to fill up our cups again, then he leaned back in his chair.

I asked Bahkti if now would be a good time to ask for

Kozlowski. Bahkti nodded and asked the king.

"Na," he answered, then took another sip from his golden cup. He added several more words.

Bahkti said, "No, he likes Kozlowski."

I said, "Tell him we would like to offer him our serving girls in exchange for Kozlowski."

Bahkti did so, at which the king brushed aside our offer and took another sip.

"He says he already has serving girls."

"Please respectfully point out that we brought back his daughter."

Bahkti said something and indicated Queenie.

The king turned toward her and grunted, "Eh? Na. Na hai," and a few more words.

Queenie jumped up, glared and pointed at him and snapped a few choice words of her own.

Bahkti said, "He says he does not want her back. She is too much trouble."

The king waved toward me and said something. Bahkti translated, "He says she is your problem now."

Queenie jabbed her finger at him—her whole arm, actually—and yelled something at him. He turned to me, pointed to her, and said something brief. Bahkti said, "He says, you see?"

While Queenie let loose another stream of invective, I asked Bahkti what he suggested we do. He replied, "We could take the women to the marketplace and see how much we can raise."

I gave him the go-ahead to negotiate for us. He asked the king how much he wanted for Kozlowski, and the king answered fifty thousand gold palms. After some consultation with me and Kozlowski, Bahkti offered five thousand, which they thought we could reasonably raise. The king seemed to enjoy the haggling, and seemed quite satisfied when the agreed price turned out to be twenty thousand gold palms. Queenie herself seemed not unsatisfied with this price. After that we bade the king a good night.

When we got back to our quarters, Chi asked me, "What about Mar-si?"

I had been debating with myself on that very question. "I don't think we can keep her, Chi. And we need to raise twenty thousand for Kozlowski."

"She won't bring much, if everyone thinks of her the way Queenie and the women do. And I like her."

"So do I, Chi, so do I."

/ / /

DAY 7 - MARKETPLACE

The next day, at the marketplace, our consignment was fourth in line. We waited patiently, watching and trying to learn from the three auctions ahead of us. The locals stared at us as we stood nonchalantly in our off-world armor, with incomprehensibly advanced weapons slung over our shoulders.

It seems that serving girls were going for two hundred gold palms and up, depending on age, strength and general appearance. In the auction ahead of ours, the bids for a real stunner shot up quickly. She was outfitted like a belly dancer, complete with little coins decorating her wrists and hips and bodice. As bids crossed eight hundred, she grinned and leaned forward and urged the bidders to go higher. When bids hit a thousand, she raised her hands over her head and hooted and shook her assets, jingling those coins for everyone to see and hear. The crowd went wild and bid her up to twenty-one hundred. When the auctioneer rang his gong, she whooped and shimmied and jingled, then she climbed down the steps and hopped into the arms of her new owner, to enthusiastic applause from the crowd.

I wondered if any of our women would be considered in her league. We had six, plus Mar-si, plus Queenie. Me, I wasn't sure if the king's daughter was really going to show up to be auctioned. It seemed bizarre that a king would allow this to happen to his daughter, but he had said she was mine, and I needed to do something to raise twenty thousand palms, so I hoped she would show.

Then it was our turn. The six women marched onto the stage one after another to enthusiastic introductions from the auctioneer. I must say, they musta been bathing and powdering and painting themselves all night, the way they shined. And it wasn't just the makeup – Each one beamed with pride, and didn't mind showing her pride to the crowd.

The auctioneer started, asking for an opening bid of five hundred for the first one. She stepped forward and displayed herself from all sides in that beauty contestant way. Bidding climbed quickly to nine hundred, then slowed to a steady rise toward a thousand. Two bidders in particular seemed determined not to let the other one have her.

As her price climbed, the crowd started to get excited again, and then she hit a thousand and she raised her hands and hooted and danced every bit as boldly as the stunner before her. The crowd went wild and bid her up to eighteen hundred and seventy five. When the auctioneer rang his gong, she threw her arms up again and shimmied her whole body, then launched herself right off the stage and into her new owner's arms. The crowd loved it and applauded, and I couldn't help but be proud of her, too.

In fact, I had good reason to be proud of all six of

them. Each seemed determined to bring in the highest price possible, and each rewarded the bidders with a little show as her price crossed a thousand. I guess Bahkti would say it was to prove their worth and to maximize their self-esteem, but the net effect was that they were helping us reach our goal for Kozlowski's release, and for that I was very grateful.

All together, our six girls brought in just over eleven thousand palms, but with a goal of twenty thousand and just Mar-si and Queenie to go, I can tell you I was getting kinda nervous.

The auctioneer changed his tone to what seemed like stand-up comedy, then called forward Mar-si. The audience laughed like they'd just heard the punch line, but as for me, I was just glad to see her again. She was all cleaned up and was wearing a plain white shift in place of her rags. Her hair had been braided, too, and I couldn't help thinking how pretty she was, and how bravely she walked out to the front of the stage, even though the crowd was pointing and jeering. She looked out over the crowd and straight into my eyes and there she paused.

I winked at her and nodded. She smiled and stood even straighter and nodded back at me.

The auctioneer pranced and swept his arm toward Mar-si and winked at the audience and started the bidding at five. Not five hundred, just five. And nobody bid.

The auctioneer bowed before the crowd and swept his arm in another arc toward Mar-si and smiled and asked for bids again. He got a bid for one palm. Well, that broke the ice, and a couple more bids got her up to six, and I can tell you my heart started to hurt for her.

Chi tapped Bahkti and said something, at which he raised his hand and bid ten.

I raised my hand and bid twenty. Evers raised his hand and bid thirty.

The crowd's mockery faded and they all turned to look at us. Chi met their stares, raised her hand, and bid fifty. I raised my hand and bid eighty. Evers made it an even hundred.

The crowd gaped at us like we were crazy. I turned to look at Mar-si, and she was beaming at us and clapping her hands and bouncing on her toes. The crowd looked at her and then back to us, and somebody must have thought they were missing out on something, because he bid a hundred and twenty.

Chi bid one fifty, I bid one eighty, and Evers bid two twenty.

Someone else must have not wanted to be left out, because he bid two forty.

Chi bid two sixty, I bid two eighty, and Evers bid three hundred.

Well, the crowd wasn't going to let us get away with whatever we were doing. Five or six of them started bidding against us and then against each other and drove Mar-si's price up to six fifty, where it hung.

Chi bid seven hundred, I bid eight hundred, and Evers bid nine. Bahkti bid nine fifty, and I bid an even thousand. Mar-si hooted and jumped up and down and hopped in a circle.

The bidders stared at us and at her, then glared at us as if we had affronted their manhood. Then they started bidding again. They got her up to fifteen fifty, and there they wavered again. Evers bid sixteen hundred, Chi bid eighteen hundred, and I bid two thousand. Mar-si hopped and hopped and ran in a circle and threw herself into the auctioneer's arms. I think he was even more astounded than the crowd was.

Well, the crowd had passed its limit of credulity. They threw their hands into the air and began to mutter to themselves and to each other. They shook their fists at each other and at the auctioneer and complained loudly. He chickened out, dropped Mar-si, and rang the gong to signal that the little dog food girl was sold. Mar-si screamed at the top of her lungs, ran toward the edge of the stage and launched herself into my arms and kissed me and flopped over into Chi's arms and hugged and kissed her and scrambled into Evers' arms and kissed him too.

The bidders threw up their hands and complained as if we had broken some taboo. It seemed a few of them were about to wash their hands of the whole mess, when a trumpet sounded and a herald announced the arrival of the king. Well, that meant they *couldn't* leave, and had to bow their heads instead.

The king strode in, accompanied by a pair of armed guards, and ascended to his covered seat at the side of the courtyard. He yelled something at the crowd to quiet them down, and sat down.

The auctioneer bowed and cleared his throat and began to describe the next ware to be auctioned. His voiced dipped low to draw the crowd in, then built and built as the grandeur of his description grew. All eyes and ears were focused on him, and then he gestured to the doorway and introduced the highlight of the morning, the incomparable daughter of the king himself.

All eyes turned toward the doorway, ours included. Queenie made her entrance, and what an entrance it was. She was clad in a gown of brilliantly colored feathers, with a feathered crown and a necklace of, you guessed it, more feathers. She swept the gown in front of herself as she walked, giving ample glimpses of what the high bidder would receive. And when she made it to the front center of the stage, she spread her arms wide, straightened her back, and struck a statuesque pose.

The crowd simply stared, dumbfounded.

The auctioneer said something majestic, motioned grandly to Queenie, and asked for a starting bid of ten thousand.

Nobody said anything—everyone was frozen in disbelief.

The auctioneer said that majestic thing again, motioned grandly again, and repeated his request for a starting bid of ten thousand. The would-be bidders looked at each other in silence, at a loss for what to do.

The king cleared his throat, leaned forward, and bid one hundred gold palms.

This Queenie could not abide. She thrust an arm at her father and wagged her finger at him and let loose with her opinion of his offer. Then she lowered her arm to sweep her finger across the crowd and gave them a few choice words too.

I didn't understand what she said, but I know a threat when I hear one. The would-be bidders must have heard one too, judging by the way they turned pale and shrank back. One of them, in the back, tentatively raised his hand and asked, "Two hundred?" Queenie yelled at him, then yelled at the crowd again. When she finished, another man, near the front, turned toward the auctioneer and, in a quavering voice, asked, "Three hundred?"

This could go on forever, I thought. I don't know much about auctions, but it's my impression that the idea is to build some momentum. So I raised my hand and offered a thousand.

Queenie turned to me and sort of stared at me, as if she didn't know what I was doing, or maybe she thought *I* didn't know what I was doing, and she would have been right. Chi looked up at me with the same sort of expression, and so did Evers. To be honest, I didn't know if this would help, or if I would end up just buying my own property back and paying the auctioneer's commission to boot. I realized there was a real chance that I would end up squandering our new-gotten wealth on this attractively attired hellion and ruin our chances of getting back Kozlowski.

In the silence that followed my bid, the king cleared his throat again and offered a thousand and twenty-five. He followed this by leaning toward the crowd, and gesturing with a sort of lifting motion of his palm, as if he was inviting competing offers.

I saw Chi, next to me, take a deep breath, then her hand shot up and she called, "Twelve hundred." She turned to me and said, "I don't know, maybe I want a wench to bring me my morning coffee."

Anyway, that broke the dam. Bids started popping up, and soon crossed five thousand, then fifty-five hundred. And there things started to peter out again. I'm sure the bidding had gotten way higher than anyone had ever paid before, and they may still have been reeling by the surreality of the whole thing.

As for me, I was wondering which would be a more valuable bargaining chip, a king's daughter or six thousand gold palms. Sure, she could be a pain in the ass, and I wouldn't want her yelling at me the way she yelled at her father or at the crowd. But she had killed those three vermin for me, I'm sure of it, and had guarded my flank when the kanora had nearly overrun us, and she had given me the credit for the kills to build me up before her father. So I raised my hand and bid six thousand.

Chi looked up at me. "She better be real good at making coffee."

The crowd fidgeted. Some of the men checked their pockets to see if they could afford to go higher, but no one bid.

I got this uneasy feeling that I'd just bought my own property and paid too much. But then the king rose and declared, in his language, "Twenty thousand palms for the girl."

The crowd, and us too, turned to the king. A sigh of relief swept the floor, me included. The auctioneer rang his gong, then rang it a bunch more to signal the end of the auction. Sanity had been restored to the kingdom, and we'd gotten our goal.

Bahkti said, "We'd better go settle up."

We got in line for the cashier. When it was our turn, Bahkti and I stepped forward and Queenie magically appeared. The cashier toted up our bill. After the six women, plus Queenie, plus and minus the two thousand for Mar-si, and then less commissions and fees, he announced our gain was twenty-nine thousand, but he would have to hold back nineteen of that until the king paid for his daughter.

Queenie told him what he could do with that idea, and demanded that we be paid now.

Reluctantly, the cashier pulled a set of wire hoops out of his pocket, each containing ten or twenty or thirty gold beads of various sizes. These he counted out and handed to us.

Queenie took them and said, "Na, ik tota," and she proceeded to flick through the beads. Apparently the count came up short, because she waved them in front of the cashier and growled something at him. He paled and gulped, pulled another hoop out of his pocket, and counted out four more beads.

I gave all of our earnings to Bahkti for safe keeping, then Queenie led me aside. With Chi watching from a distance, and Queenie holding my right arm, Queenie placed the palm of her hand on my breastplate, then placed it on her own breast, and asked in her language, "Six thousand?"

I couldn't tell if she was feeling insulted or was happy about it. I remember that, early on, she had claimed to be worth ten thousand palms, but maybe that was just her opening position. So I simply looked her in the eyes and nodded. The corners of her lips turned up and her eyes twinkled and she formed a little kiss on her lips, and then she winked. I guess she was happy with the deal after all.

/ / /

FINAL BARGAIN

That evening we dined with the king again. I passed on the eyeballs this time. Queenie didn't seem to mind. I suppose it left more for her and her father.

After dinner, he motioned that our cups be filled again, and then we got down to business. Bahkti counted out twenty thousand palms and handed them to the king, who riffled through them to make sure the count was right. Then he announced that he needed a hundred more for the commission.

Queenie sprang up and protested, but he raised his palm to her and said he had to pay a commission to buy his daughter, so we would have to pay a commission to buy Kozlowski. I gave Bahkti the nod, figuring it was a small price to pay to maintain good will.

The blushing girl followed us back to our quarters, where she busied herself straightening out the bedding and fluffing pillows. I figured she was either a spy or she just liked to be near Kozlowski.

Chi asked me, "You took quite a chance there, Boss, bidding six thousand for Queenie. How did you know the king would come through?"

"I didn't. But it seemed unlikely that he would allow his offspring to be disrespected by a low price, or that he would let her become the property of a commoner, or worse yet, an off-worlder. I had to believe this was all just his way of humbling her, to take her down a notch or two."

Bahkti interjected, "I think it was a wise move. We stood to earn less than sixteen thousand as it was, after paying the auction fees. Not enough to buy Koz. It was worth the gamble that her father would intercede."

Chi asked, "What're you going to do with the other seven thousand?"

"I thought I might go to the marketplace again tomorrow, just to make sure that freckles are selling for a decent price."

Bahkti shook his head. "I would urge restraint. We don't want to increase the value of other tribespeople, because that would make it more profitable to kidnap them."

Damn, I hadn't thought of that.

Chi said, "We got to do something. I don't like the message it sends when they're considered essentially worthless."

I said, "Well, maybe we can come up with a price that increases their worth but doesn't make it profitable to steal them."

Bahkti spread his palms. "We can certainly go see what we can do."

Kozlowski came over. "Uh, Baker, you know that fifty I owe you? Well, I was wondering, since you're flush with dough-re-mi, if you could lend me a couple hundred palms. I've been thinking of making a little investment down here."

I glanced past him at the woman gently brushing dust from our supply pack and asked if the investment was the kind that blushed.

He nodded.

"Well, then you'll need a thousand. That seems to be the magic number to show you value someone."

"Could you? That'd be great. And maybe a little more to make a down-payment on an apartment."

I sighed, and had Bahkti count out two thousand palms.

/ / /

DAY 8 - THE PRICE OF DOG FOOD

The next morning, we five and Mar-si made our way to the marketplace. Mar-si, Chi and Bahkti made a detour past some stalls selling clothing, where they picked out a nice dress for Mar-si and a souvenir veil for Chi. The proprietress let Mar-si step behind a curtain, and when she came out, she didn't look like a rag girl or a slave girl, she looked like, well, a regular, well-dressed girl.

When they rejoined us, Mar-si threw her arms wide and twirled to show off her new dress, then she hugged me and hugged Chi again. I reached in my pocket and pulled out one of the hoops of gold beads and called her to me and knelt and fastened the hoop around her neck, so then she looked like a young woman of means. She beamed and patted it and hugged me again.

The auctions were in progress. I'm guessing news of yesterday's events had circulated throughout the city, because there were several freckles-and-russet women and even an auburn up for sale. They were going for fifty to two hundred palms, which certainly seemed a lot better than the six that had been offered for Mar-si yesterday. Bahkti cautioned us against raising their prices much further.

The next ware to be sold was also a freckles-and-russet. Mar-si's mouth popped open, and she grabbed Chi's arm and started hopping up and down and pointing. Bahkti translated. "She says it is her cousin."

Mar-si pulled the hoop off from around her neck and held it up for Bahkti, then pointed at her cousin. I told him, "We got more if you need it."

We paid three fifty for her. I'm sure the price was so high because it was obvious that Bahkti was fronting for off-worlders, but the price was worth it when the girl climbed down and rushed into Mar-si's arms.

/ / /

GOODBYE

I stood on the observation deck of our ship. We were due to pull out of orbit in just a few minutes, and I wanted to get one last look at Tashara, below. I heard the door at the other end whisk open and close, and I heard footsteps walk lightly toward me. I looked to my right, and it was Chi. She took the window next to mine.

We stared at the little golden planet for some time, then Chi asked, "Did Phillips like your report?"

"No. He said it was too short. Lacked detail. Did he like yours?"

"No. Same reason."

I thought about the bones of three dead locals down on Tashara, and I thought about the eight women we had sold, and the girls we had bought. Those were just a few of the details that didn't make it into my report. Since I hadn't been called on the carpet yet, I guessed that those details hadn't made it into Chi's or Evers' or Bahkti's reports, either, so I said, "Thanks."

"No problem," said Chi.

We both stared out the window for a while, then Chi said, "I hope Koz likes it down there."

"I think he will. He'll do just fine, particularly with a native wife. And the king said he likes him."

Chi said, "Yeah. Phillips was sure quick to okay it. He's been looking for tribes to establish relations with, and Koz is just the guy to make it happen."

A little while later, she added, "I told him Mar-si's tribe ought to work out, too."

"So did I."

By the way, you might like to know that we transported Mar-si and her cousin back home. Their parents were sure glad to see them again, all dressed in fine clothing and each wearing a necklace of gold beads. We made their families each pay us a yak for them, a high price for a woman in their culture, but the girls had sentimental value, I suppose, and the girls' new-found wealth more than made up for their high price. Before we left, we gave each family the other's yak as a thank-you for their hospitality.

Chi interrupted my thoughts. "Your contract is up in four months, isn't it?"

"Yeah."

"You gonna re-up?"

"I don't know. Been thinking about cashing out, maybe joining a private security service. When the Territorial Office sets up a legation to a new planet, they usually hire private contractors to handle security."

Chi asked, "You thinking anyplace special?"

"Yeah. Someplace where experience counts."

The ship slowly turned, and Tashara started to drop away from us. Chi said, "My date's three months after yours. If you get set up, you call me, okay? Unless your hands 're gonna be full, that is."

Well fine, I thought. "I don't think my hands'll be full."

"Then you call me, okay? I mean it. You might need someone to, you know, watch your flank or something."

"If you mean it, Chi, then you'll be the first one I call."

She glanced at me, but looked away kind of nervously. She said, "Well, I do. Mean it, I mean."

I pulled her to my side and wrapped an arm around her shoulders. She put an arm around my waist. I think neither of us was quite comfortable with this right now or right here—there's not enough privacy on this ship—so we let each other go.

She cleared her throat and pulled a modest distance away, then turned to look out the window. Her voice came kind of quietly, "Like I said, you call."

I turned to look out the window too. Tashara's sun shrank away as our ship slipped into hyperdrive. I said, "Okay, copy that."

/ / / / /

Bargain Princess

OTHER BOOKS BY PEYTON REESE

Cassie to the Coast — a "boy meets girl" adventure set in present-day Oregon, USA. Released Febuary 2015. Turn this page for a short sample.

See www.PeytonReese.com for information and links to the electronic versions.

/ / /

In addition, Peyton has assisted with **The Marguerite Series**, a love story set in Central Europe in the late 1800's. For more information, visit the series web site, www.JessicaWillowby.com

/ / / / /

Cassie to the Coast

A guy-meets-girl love story set in present-day Oregon

Excerpt:

Cassandra, next to me, muttered something in her sleep. Whatever she was dreaming, it wasn't good. A second later she shouted "No!" and sat half upright.

She blinked and looked around and saw me. Her cap had fallen off while she slept, and her hair looked kind of wild and she seemed a little disoriented. She looked kind of cute that way. I smiled.

She grabbed the rear-view mirror and twisted it to look into it, then ran her fingers through her hair until it was mostly orderly, and then she found her cap and jammed it back onto her head. "Seen enough?" she challenged.

No, I thought. I guess she didn't like being caught with her guard down.

I did notice, though, as she was straightening her hair, that her left ear had about six piercings, but only the bottom one had an earring in it. I wondered if she'd lost the others, or if she'd outgrown them.

To put her at ease, or to start a conversation or something, I asked, "You have a bad dream?"

She looked at me, trying to decide if she should answer, I guess, then she said "Yeah," and turned her attention out the right-side window, to shut me out I suppose.

We were following a motor home down a winding section of roadway, again not unusual for the coast range. She turned to me and said, "Do you ever dream about dying?"

I looked at her. "No. Do you?"

She looked out the front window. "Yeah. All the time." There was a pause, and then she added, "I don't sleep so good."

She didn't elaborate. I wondered, *What am I, a magnet for nuts or something?* Some guys are chick magnets, I'm a nut magnet.

She turned to look at me, then she pulled her arm out from her shoulder belt and slowly reached over and put her fingers on my chest, right over my heart, and then she pressed her whole hand flat onto me. I glanced down as she did this, but I said nothing.

She took her hand away slowly and closed her fingers as if she wanted to not lose something. Then she asked, "If you were going to die, would you want to be warned ahead of time?"

"Well, yeah, sure. Then I could do something about it, so that it wouldn't happen."

"So then, something you would do would prevent you from dying, at least in that way, and you would live longer, and later die some other way. Because all of us, all of us are going to die some day."

I glanced at her. *Oh, great. Nuttier and nuttier.*

She was looking right at me when I thought this, and I hoped she couldn't see what I was thinking.

She said, quite calmly, as if to allay my fear, "It's not *me* who is going to kill you. Not today."

...

Cassie to the Coast is a novella-length love story, approximately 37500 words, 31 chapters.

Explore → www.PeytonReese.com